Dear Parents:

Children learn to read in stages, and all children develop reading skills at different ages. **Ready Readers**™ were created to promote children's interest in reading and to increase their reading skills. **Ready Readers**™ are written on two levels to accommodate children ranging in age from three through eight. These stages are meant to be used only as a guide.

Stage 1: Preschool-Grade 1
Stage 1 books are written in very short, simple sentences with large type. They are perfect for children who are getting ready to read or are just becoming familiar with reading on their own.

Stage 2: Grades 1-3
Stage 2 books have longer sentences and are a bit more complex. They are suitable for children who are able to read but still may need help.

All the **Ready Readers**™ tell varied, easy-to-follow stories and are colorfully illustrated. Reading will be fun, and soon your child will not only be ready, but eager to read.

Tommy Stays Up Late

Written by Eugene Bradley Coco
Illustrated by Robert Sabuda

Modern Publishing
A Division of Unisystems, Inc.
New York, New York 10022

Tommy had a busy day.
He went to school.

He played in the park.

He did his homework,

and he cleaned up his room.

Now it was time to go to sleep.

But Tommy was not tired.

He decided to stay up late
and watch the sun rise.

Tommy took his pillow.

He took his blanket,

and he took his favorite bear.

Tommy even took his flashlight.

Then Tommy put his chair
by the window.

He looked at the sky.

It was very dark.

He looked at the stars.
They were very bright.

He looked at the moon.

It was very big.

Soon Tommy started to get tired.

He rubbed his eyes.

Tommy let out a great big yawn.

"I must stay up," thought Tommy.
"The sun will rise soon."

But Tommy fell asleep.

Suddenly, Tommy heard
his mother calling.

"Wake up, Tommy," she said.

Tommy opened his eyes.

It was morning but it was
still dark outside.

The sun had waited for Tommy.